HELLO KITTY
and friends

The Pop Princess

HELLO KITTY

and friends

The Pop Princess

HarperCollins *Children's Books*

MEET HELLO KITTY
and friends

Hello Kitty

Mimmy

Tammy

Mama

Papa

Grandpa

Grandma

Fifi

Dear Daniel

With special thanks to
Linda Chapman and Michelle Misra

First published in Great Britain by HarperCollins *Children's Books* in 2013

www.harpercollins.co.uk
1 3 5 7 9 10 8 6 4 2
ISBN: 978-000-751439-7

Printed and bound in England by Clays Ltd, St Ives plc.

Contents

Super-Cool News

It was Saturday, and Hello Kitty hummed as she arranged her lip balms in a row and then lined up her hair bows on her desk. Finally she sorted out her pens and pencils, putting the pink ones – her favourite colour – right at the front. There!

She sat back. Her desk looked just right!

She heard the sound of running feet on the landing and then her bedroom door flew open. Her twin sister Mimmy burst in, gasping. She looked like she was about to **POP** with excitement. What could the good news be?

Mimmy jumped up and down in excitement as she told Hello Kitty that their favourite band in the whole wide world, the Fizzy Pops, were having an open-air concert in the park in two weeks' time and Mama said that they could both go! **Hooray!**

Hello Kitty grabbed her sister's hands and they spun each other round. The Fizzy Pops were the best pop group ever! This was SUPER news!

Mama had also told Mimmy that they could take a picnic to the concert. She was on the phone right now buying two tickets.

Hello Kitty felt happiness rush through her all the way from her toes to her head. They could make *special* food and take the big pink and blue picnic rug and dance and sing along with the songs. It would be so much fun! Suddenly she knew what would make it even more fun… what if Fifi, Tammy and Dear Daniel could come too?

 The Pop Princess

Fifi, Tammy and Dear Daniel were her really good friends – such good friends that they had formed a club called **The Friendship Club**. They had membership cards and a password, and had meetings at each other's houses where they played games and made things. They also thought up rules about friendship.

Friendship Club Rules

1. Good Friends come in all shapes and sizes.
2. Good friends make hard things easy to do!
3. Good friends like you just the way you are!

Mimmy didn't join them all the time as she had friends of her own too, but she liked being part of the Friendship Club meetings if she was around.

For the concert it would be the more the merrier, Mimmy said, smiling – and then her eyes widened. That had given her a **great** idea! She told Hello Kitty about an article she'd read in *Pop Girl* magazine last month. It said that sometimes when the Fizzy Pops performed they chose groups of people from the audience who were dancing really well to appear on stage with them.

Hello Kitty imagined being chosen and her stomach fluttered with excitement. The girls both hugged themselves with happiness,

but then Mimmy had a thought. They would probably only choose older girls and boys to actually go on stage, she said. But they would still have lots of fun!

Hello Kitty agreed – it would be fun no matter what, but they should still practise dancing, just in case! Suddenly one of her special, super, Hello Kitty ideas popped into her head. She could ask Mama if she could have a Friendship Club meeting after lunch. Then she could tell her

friends about the concert, and everyone could

rehearse together!

What a *super* day this was turning out

to be!

Practice Makes Perfect

Hello Kitty rang her friends to invite them over

and then she and Mimmy set about getting

the lounge ready for a **special** Fizzy Pops

Friendship Club meeting. First of all, they stuck

up posters of the Fizzy Pops on the walls. There

were three girls in the band — Tawana, Sita and Mia. Tawana had dark hair, Sita had red hair and Mia had blonde hair. They had been friends since school. Hello Kitty knew **everything** about them, from their favourite foods to their favourite colours.

Mimmy sighed as she looked up at the posters. Being on stage with the Fizzy Pops would be a dream come true. She plumped up the cushions and turned on their music. Making up a dance routine would be fun!

Then Mimmy had a great idea. She called out to Hello Kitty, who was *singing* along to the music. They should make some cupcakes in

Tawana, Sita and Mia's favourite colours for the meeting! She had also read in *Pop Girl* about the Fizzy Pops' favourite cupcake flavours — Tawana liked strawberry, Sita liked lemon and Mia liked chocolate.

Mama helped them as they measured out the ingredients and whisked them all together.

They waited for the cakes to cook and cool and then carefully iced them. As they worked, they sang along to one of the Fizzy Pops' songs. Hello Kitty pretended the wooden spoon was a microphone and Mimmy had a spatula, and as they sang they worked out some dance steps to Hello Kitty's favourite song: *Sunshine Girl.*

Mama smiled as she watched them. She could see how **excited** they were about the concert! She asked if their friends liked the Fizzy Pops as much as they did. Hello Kitty and Mimmy both nodded and started talking at once – everyone loved The Fizzy Pops! But out of all of the friends, Hello Kitty and Mimmy liked them the most.

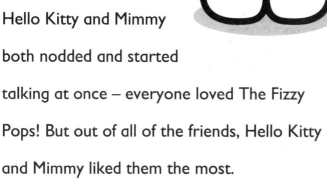

Hello Kitty knew that Tammy was a Fizzy Pops fan and that Dear Daniel and Fifi had other favourite bands. But when Hello Kitty had phoned her friends and told them the news, Dear Daniel and Fifi had been just as keen to come to the concert as Tammy had been. It was going to be a **great** Friendship Club day out!

At last the cakes were ready, their tops thick with gooey icing and sprinkles. Hello Kitty arranged them on a plate and put them in the lounge, and then

the doorbell rang. Her heart leapt. The meeting

was about to begin!

Tammy nearly fell though the

door, she was so *excited*.

She spun into the hallway,

singing the chorus from

Sunshine Girl.

She and Dear Daniel had never been to a concert before at all, so they were super-thrilled.

Everyone chattered together – they all hoped that they would be picked to dance on stage at the concert. But it would still be **brilliant** fun, even if they didn't get chosen! Hello Kitty mentioned that she thought the best way to impress the band was to do a dance routine. She put on *Sunshine Girl* and turned the music up, then organised everyone into a line and began to show them some steps.

First she stepped to the right, then she stepped to the left, and then she put her hands

in the air and **spun** round. The Friendship Club copied her dance moves. Once everyone was dancing in time with each other Hello Kitty added some more steps to the routine. She counted them in from the beginning again.

And a one, two, three and four…

They were all doing really well, quickly picking the steps up and singing along too.

"I see you over the road so I cross and hold your hand,

For you I'd walk to the ends of the land!"

After half an hour they were all very warm from so much dancing and singing, but they had the dance routine to *Sunshine Girl* all worked out. They stopped to take a break.

Hello Kitty handed round the **delicious** cupcakes and some of Mama's homemade lemonade. That was one song done – now they just needed to practise another one too. Mimmy

suggested that they should do a routine to

Falling Star; she had read in *Pop Girl* that the

Fizzy Pops always played this song at their concerts, so they would definitely get a chance to dance to it.

Dear Daniel *flopped* on to the cushions. Could they please learn the second routine another day, he asked – he was worn out!

Tammy also sat down,
fanning herself. She
was tired too. Fifi
pointed out that
there was lots to
decide, apart from

the dance routine – like

what food they should take for the picnic.

Hello Kitty fetched her pad and pencil and

as everyone called out their suggestions, she

started to make a list of the food they should

take to the concert, as well as other things they

would need, like a picnic rug. She also worked

out a rehearsal schedule to practise the dances.

But what could they do for now? Hmmm…

Mimmy had a super idea! They could do a

quiz about the Fizzy Pops. There were some

questions in her *Pop Girl* magazine!

By the time everyone's parents came to

collect them, the Friendship Club had had a

really good meeting. It had been so much fun planning their outing and asking each other questions about the band, and everything was all worked out now, from their next practice all the way until the concert. Fifi and Tammy were very impressed. Hello Kitty was the best at organising things. How did she do it, they asked? Hello Kitty giggled, and told them her secret was just writing lists!

She also **l♥ved** organising things for her friends. Tammy and Fifi looked at each other and grinned.

They knew they were lucky to have a friend like Hello Kitty. It would be nice to surprise her by organising something themselves one day.

The Friendship Club waved goodbye to each other, and that night Hello Kitty went to bed feeling very **happy**. They'd agreed to meet after school on Monday to practise. They wanted their dance routines to be perfect for the concert! Hello Kitty shut her eyes. She could almost imagine she was there, right at

the front of the concert and about to be asked
go on stage with all her friends. If *only*
her daydream could come true! Lost in happy
thoughts, she fell asleep.

Forgetful Friends

It was Monday morning and Hello Kitty ran

across the playground to where Tammy and

Dear Daniel were standing. She'd been busy

the night before, making up more dance

moves for the second routine and couldn't

wait to share them with her friends! Quickly,

she checked that they were still coming to the

Friendship Club meeting after school.

Dear Daniel **gasped**.

He'd forgotten that he

had football practice!

He looked really

sorry. But Tammy

could still go…

Hello Kitty smiled

at Dear Daniel. She

reassured him

that he was not to worry and that

she'd teach him the steps at the

next rehearsal, on Thursday. But Dear Daniel had Nature Club on Thursdays! The only day he could meet was Saturday. It would only give them a week to practise but that should still be enough time if they worked hard. **Oh well!**

They heard Fifi calling out and looked
round to see her racing across the playground
towards them. Her bag was flapping and her
hair had escaped from its ponytail, and she
was breathing heavily from running so fast.

Fifi went to ice-skating lessons before school so she was often in a rush to get there on time, especially at the moment as she was learning a new routine for a competition. Her coach was trying to teach her a new spin. It was really hard but she had almost got it right that morning! Hopefully she'd do it properly when she went back to the ice rink after school.

It seemed Fifi had forgotten about the rehearsal for the Fizzy Pops concert too! Hello Kitty reminded her and Fifi clapped her hand to her mouth. *Oh no!* But it was too late to rearrange her ice-skating lesson.

Hello Kitty told her it didn't matter – Dear Daniel couldn't come either. They would all meet on Saturday and practise the second routine then. And Hello Kitty, Tammy and Mimmy would still practise that night so they could get a head start for Saturday. It would be fine!

Fifi hugged Hello Kitty and thanked her for not minding. She promised to work **extra** hard on Saturday, and so did Dear Daniel.

Just then, the morning bell rang. Everyone rushed to be first in line! Putting the thoughts of the rehearsal out of her mind, Hello Kitty ran after her friends.

After school that day, Mimmy and Tammy were following Hello Kitty's new dance moves. They reached to the side, jumped back, put their arms up and turned to the left. This was when they would dance with their partners! Mimmy would dance with Dear Daniel, Tammy would be with Fifi and Hello Kitty would be in the middle, **dancing** by herself.

Hello Kitty watched as Mimmy and Tammy pretended to turn Dear Daniel and Fifi around. *Hmmm...* It didn't look quite right. It was hard to tell if it looked good without the others being there!

Hello Kitty paused the music and Tammy and Mimmy stopped dancing while she explained her thinking. They decided to try the routine

again on Saturday, when Dear Daniel and Fifi
would be there. Suddenly Mimmy had an idea!
Just because they couldn't dance, it didn't mean
they couldn't get ready for the concert in other
ways. They would need costumes, right, she
guessed?

Costumes! Hello Kitty's eyes lit up. She couldn't believe she hadn't thought about that yet! She adored designing clothes and making outfits. **Yes, yes, yes,** she declared – they would definitely need costumes! Mimmy and Tammy clapped their hands with happiness. They might not be able to practise their dancing but making costumes was just as

much fun! Hello Kitty grabbed some paper and pencils and sat down at the table to think. What could they wear for the concert? It had to be something sparkly,

something cool, something totally

SUPER!

Mimmy and Tammy went into the kitchen to get some drinks and snacks while Hello Kitty started to plan the costumes. They couldn't wait to see what she'd come up with!

An hour later the tabletop in the lounge was covered with costume designs and cookie crumbs. Tammy's *favourite* design was a black leotard with silver stars all over it. Hello Kitty liked this too, but she wanted everyone to look the same and she was pretty sure Dear Daniel wouldn't want to wear a leotard! Mimmy and Tammy giggled at the thought.

They looked at all the drawings again. Another design was black trousers for Dear Daniel and a sticky-out black skirt for the girls. They could all wear

customised T-shirts that had 'Fizzy Pops' written on them in rainbow-coloured sparkly letters. Mimmy announced that this one was her favourite, and they all looked at each other, smiling. Perfect – all three girls loved it! Now they just had to make the costumes.

HELLO KITTY *and friends*

Hello Kitty beamed at her friends. Making costumes was one of her favourite things to do – it would be so much **FUN!** They just needed some white T-shirts to draw the design on to with glitter fabric pens. Hello Kitty could make

the skirts out of some old ballet tutus that she

and Mimmy had in their dressing-up cupboard.

Tammy clapped her hands. She couldn't wait

to get started!

4

Saturday's Rehearsal

Hello Kitty sang *Sunshine Girl* as she carried the

flapjacks she had made into the lounge. She'd

already put drinks out, turned the music on

and cleared a space on the floor so they could

all rehearse their dances. They needed a lot

more practice, but at least it was the

weekend and they had all day!

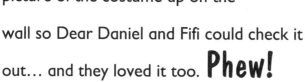

At eleven o'clock, everyone

arrived. Hello Kitty had stuck the

picture of the costume up on the

wall so Dear Daniel and Fifi could check it

out… and they loved it too. **Phew!**

Hello Kitty beamed. She was pleased that

everyone liked her design. She explained that

she'd made the skirts; Dear Daniel

could wear his school

trousers, and Mama

had bought plain white

T-Shirts for everyone

so they could add the

sparkly lettering after

they'd finished rehearsing

and had lunch. But Dear Daniel piped up that

he couldn't stay that long – his dad was taking

him to the Natural History Museum. He hadn't

realised they would be busy all day!

The Pop Princess

Hello Kitty looked at him in alarm. *Oh no!*

There wouldn't be time to make the costumes

and practise two dances all before lunch. Fifi

quietly said that she also couldn't stay for long.

She had to be at the ice rink by lunchtime. And

Mimmy had an extra flute lesson too.

Hello Kitty sighed. Today was supposed to be their big practising session, and there was no way they could learn both dances before lunch. Tomorrow she and Mimmy were out with their grandparents, so that only left after school and it was always hard to meet then because of people having after-school clubs. And what about making the T-shirts?

Dear Daniel was **really** sorry, and so were Fifi and Mimmy. They tried to make Hello Kitty feel better by telling her how exciting

being at the concert together would be, even if they didn't get chosen to go on stage.

Hello Kitty knew this was true, but she was still a bit disappointed. The Fizzy Pops were here favourite band ever and she *had* really wanted to go on stage. But she didn't want to make a fuss about it to her friends – especially when they couldn't help being so busy. She took a deep breath, looked up and gave them all a big smile.

Tammy glanced at her quickly, and then clapped her

hands and got everyone in a line so they could

start practising. She turned up the music and

they started with the routine they'd learned

the weekend before. Everyone remembered

Sunshine Girl very well but they had only got

halfway through learning the new routine for

Falling Star when Dear Daniel, Fifi and Mimmy all had to leave. Hello Kitty said goodbye to Dear Daniel and Fifi, and shut the door.

Tammy knew that Hello Kitty was disappointed; she knew how important the concert was to her! But she *wished* Hello Kitty had spoken up; She was sure Dear Daniel

and Fifi would have arranged another rehearsal

if they knew. She thought hard about how to

cheer Hello Kitty up. *Hmmm...* They could

finish the costumes together! If they worked

hard they could customise all five T-Shirts that

afternoon, she suggested. Mimmy could help

too when she got back from her flute lesson – it

would be fun!

Hello Kitty smiled. Tammy was right — it *would* be fun! She ran upstairs to get the T-Shirts and the glitter pens. Their costumes were going to look **super-cool!**

5

Getting Ready

When Mimmy came back from her lesson,

she joined in with the T-shirt painting. They

stopped for a **delicious** lunch and then

carried on. By teatime, all five T-shirts had been

painted so that they said 'The Fizzy Pops' in

big **sparkly** letters, and on the back of each was a large silver star. Hello Kitty had made hair bows for all the girls out of some silver ribbon, and

Mimmy and Tammy had woven bracelets from silver and black cord. They looked at everything carefully laid out on the table – it all looked great! The Friendship Club would be wearing the most stylish costumes at the concert.

Mimmy and Tammy thanked Hello Kitty for being such a super designer, and she smiled. Now that the costumes were finished she was feeling excited again about the concert.

But Tammy knew that Hello Kitty would be even happier if she was picked to go on stage.

She cleared her throat, and told Hello Kitty that she should speak to Dear Daniel and Fifi and tell them how much it meant to her. Hello Kitty shook her head. She didn't

want to bother her busy friends! She announced again how much **FUN** the concert would be, even if they didn't get chosen to dance on the stage with the Fizzy Pops. But Tammy knew Hello Kitty still felt a bit sad that Dear Daniel and Fifi hadn't had the time to learn the routine. She thought about how Hello Kitty was always doing nice things for her friends — she wanted to make the concert really special for her! So Tammy asked Hello Kitty to teach her and Mimmy the end of the routine to *Falling Star*

 anyway. It would be good if the three of them knew it, even if the others didn't.

Mimmy nodded and smiled. That was a **great** idea!

Hello Kitty switched the music back on and showed them the last steps to the routine. They were all laughing by the end and Hello Kitty was feeling much happier. They had so much fun! Afterwards, they started tidying up.

Tammy and Mimmy went in to the kitchen to wash up the paint brushes. But when Hello Kitty offered to help too, Tammy quickly said no. She told Hello Kitty she should stay in the

living room and clear away the scraps of fabric

instead! Then she grabbed the dirty brushes and

dragged Mimmy away.

Hello Kitty was puzzled. What was going

on? Wondering to herself, she tidied the ribbon,

fabric and cord away and then went into the

kitchen. She heard

Tammy talking to

Mimmy but when

they realised Hello Kitty was there they quickly

hushed. Hello Kitty knew something was going

on – *but what?*

All that week, Hello Kitty tried to get her

friends together to practise but they always

seemed to have other things to do. Still, going

to the concert to have fun

with her friends

was the most

important

thing! When

school finished

on Friday, they all arranged to meet the next

day for the concert. Hello Kitty suggested two

o'clock in the park. That would give

them plenty of time before the

concert started.

Everyone agreed. They were

all so excited about the concert,

especially Dear Daniel and Fifi. They kept

grinning at Tammy and giggling.

Hello Kitty smiled too but all week she'd had

the feeling that there was **something**

happening that her friends weren't telling her

about! She kept catching them whispering and

then they would break off and stop when she

went up to them. As she got in to Mama's car,

she looked back at her friends who were still

all huddled together, talking quietly. Something

was definitely going on…

On Saturday, Hello Kitty put on her T-shirt and skirt, fluffing out the layers of the tutu. She slipped on the bracelet, fixed the silver bow in her hair and picked up a pot of lip balm. It **sparkled** with silver glitter. She rubbed some on her lips and then brushed just a little silver eye shadow on her eyelids. She didn't usually wear much make-up as Mama and Papa didn't like it, but they wouldn't

mind for a pop concert! Hello Kitty checked

her nails. She had already painted them with

pink sparkly polish. She took one last look in

the mirror – ready to **go!** Mimmy was already

dressed and in the kitchen, helping Mama and

Papa pack up the hamper for the picnic.

Hello Kitty spun round and Papa caught her in his arms. Her gave her a kiss on the head and remarked with a smile that she and Mimmy looked lovely.

As they drove towards the concert Hello Kitty's tummy started fluttering. Today was going to be super-cool!

The Pop Princess

6

The Fizzy Pops!

They arrived at the park, got out and went through the gates. A **large** stage stood in the middle of the grounds. There were already a lot of people there, sitting on picnic blankets and waiting for the concert to start. Hello Kitty

looked about. Where were her friends?

She stared as she suddenly caught sight of a

large banner stretched between two posts. Big

sparkly letters spelled out the words:

THE FRIENDSHIP CLUB!

Fifi, Dear Daniel and Tammy were standing

beside it – they were all in their costumes,

waving at her! **Wow!** Hello Kitty gasped in surprise. She hadn't known her friends were making a banner!

Mimmy squeezed her sister's hand and smiled. She'd been part of the secret plan and was thrilled that Hello Kitty liked it.

The banner had been Tammy's idea but it was only part of the surprise…

Hello Kitty and Mimmy ran over to the group and Tammy pressed the play button on her music player.

Falling Star flooded out. Tammy, Fifi and Dear Daniel got into line, Mimmy joined them and before Hello Kitty knew what was happening, they started performing the routine she had made up. But not just the beginning – they did the whole dance and they did it *perfectly!*

Her mouth dropped open.

She couldn't believe it!

Her friends all knew the

dance she had wanted to

teach them. When had they

had time to learn that? It was

the **best** surprise she could have ever had!

Hello Kitty hugged her friends.

Tammy beamed. She explained that she'd told Fifi and Dear Daniel how much Hello Kitty had wanted to dance onstage. They had all wanted to do their best to make it happen, so they had met at Tammy's house on Thursday and Friday. Mimmy had gone too to help Tammy teach the others the second routine. They had practised and practised until it was *perfect!*

Dear Daniel gave Hello Kitty another hug and said that he would have changed his plans if he'd known how important the concert was to her. And Fifi put in that it had been Tammy's idea to make it a surprise, as she wanted to say thank you to Hello Kitty for being such a good friend and always organising everything. Hello Kitty beamed at Tammy, who blushed happily. Hello Kitty felt so happy she thought she would float away!

She couldn't believe her friends had gone to so much trouble just for her. It made her feel very, very special. What a super surprise!

Tammy pressed play again and the music started from the beginning. This time Hello Kitty danced as well. They were all perfectly in time and ended with a final spin and cheer.

As the music stopped they heard the sound of clapping. A lady had been watching them, and as she came over she declared that they looked fantastic! Her name was Daisy and she was the Fizzy Pops' manager. She told the Friendship Club that she was looking for some people to go up on stage to dance for a few songs. She thought they would be *perfect* and asked if they'd like to do it!

Hello Kitty was so stunned she couldn't speak.

Fifi stepped forward quickly and told Daisy that they would l♥ve to dance on the stage.

Daisy smiled then asked where everyone's parents were – she would need to ask their permission. Hello Kitty pointed to where their parents were setting out the food on picnic blankets, and Daisy walked towards them and started chatting.

Hello Kitty turned to her friends. She was speechless with delight. Fifi and Mimmy squealed, and Dear Daniel and Tammy jumped up and down with excitement.

Everyone high-fived! Dancing on the stage would be **AMAZING!**

The concert started. As the band came on to the stage and played their first song, Daisy told the Friendship Club to go backstage with her. The stage-crew was there – a group of men and women dressed all in black who were hurrying round in charge of the sound and lighting. Daisy explained that when *Falling Star* began to play she wanted them to *run* on to the stage and dance just as they had done before. After that it would be *Sunshine Girl*, and then there would be another

few songs before the band took a break.

HELLO KITTY *and friends*

Hello Kitty and her friends waited nervously in the wings at the side of the stage, gripping each other's hands. The sound of cheering was deafening as the band finished their song.

 The Pop Princess

As the first notes of *Falling Star* played Daisy ushered the **Friendship Club** on to the stage. Hello Kitty took a deep breath and ran into the spotlight with all her friends following.

It was brilliant! They danced while the

Fizzy Pops sang. The audience cheered and

screamed, and they got all their steps right.

The time seemed to pass in a blur and Hello

Kitty couldn't believe it when it

was time to come off for

the break. Daisy was

waiting for them. She was

clapping, along with the

stage crew.

Hello Kitty was out of breath,

her cheeks were pink and her eyes were

shining. She felt incredible! Just when

she thought things couldn't get any better the

Fizzy Pops suddenly walked towards them. Tawana, Sita and Mia told the Friendship Club how brilliant they'd looked on stage and how impressed they were with the outfits. They smiled warmly at everyone.

Once again, Hello Kitty was lost for words. Luckily, Fifi wasn't! She told the Fizzy Pops that Hello Kitty was their biggest fan and that she'd made all the costumes, *and* made up the dance routines.

The Fizzy Pops thought that was brilliant! They told Hello Kitty that they thought she had a great future ahead of her as a fashion designer or a dance teacher. Hello Kitty couldn't believe she was talking to the Fizzy Pops. It was her dream come **true!** But she didn't want to take all the credit and told them that she couldn't have done anything without the Friendship Club to help.

After Hello Kitty mentioned it, the Fizzy Pops wanted to know all about the Friendship Club! So she explained to them

about their meetings and the Friendship Club rules and how much fun they had together. The Fizzy Pops thought it sounded fantastic! And… they used to have a club called The Perfect Pals, when they were in school! Wow! Sita even said that maybe the Friendship Club would have its own band one day too. Hello Kitty hoped so!

Daisy told everyone that the second half of the concert was about to begin. The Fizzy Pops waved goodbye and *hurried* off to get changed. Daisy gave the Friendship Club signed posters and postcards of the band and then she took them all back to their parents. And it was time for the concert to start again!

The Fizzy Pops ran out to the sound of excited cheers. They were going to play their new song called *Friends Are For Ever!* Tawana's voice was loud and clear as she spoke into the microphone. She wanted to dedicate the song to a VERY special group of friends…

The Friendship Club!

Sita and Mia pointed to where Hello Kitty and the others were in the audience and then burst into song. Swinging round with Mimmy, Hello Kitty thought that she had never been happier!

Everyone was chatting as they walked back to the car park after the concert had ended. They still couldn't believe that they'd danced on stage and met the Fizzy Pops!

Hello Kitty looked round at all her friends. She knew that they wouldn't have been picked if her friends hadn't practised so hard. She gave

them all an enormous hug and said thank you. It had been the best day ever.

Fifi and Dear Daniel agreed – they'd had so much fun – and they would have practised even more if they'd known how important the concert was to Hello Kitty from the start. Hello Kitty blushed as she realised she should have talked to her friends. Tammy nudged Hello Kitty and smiled. It was OK as it had given them a chance to **surprise** her, and it was nice to make each other feel happy, she said – that's what friends are for!

Mimmy linked arms with Hello Kitty and grinned at her.

Hello Kitty felt a warm glow. She really **did** have the most wonderful friends, and sister. In fact, she announced, it was time for a new Friendship Club rule:

You can tell a good friend anything!

Everyone cheered. It would be perfect!

Tammy suggested they all meet the next day

and add the new rule to their list. They could also listen to the Fizzy Pops and make picture frames to put their signed postcards in. And there was *always* time to bake more cakes!

Everyone laughed as they raced back to the cars. And as she ran, Hello Kitty thought to herself that there was nothing she'd rather do than spend the next day with her friends. Super!

The end

Turn over the page for activities and
fun things that you can do with your
friends – just like Hello Kitty!

Dance, dance, dance!

Hello Kitty and The Friendship Club love to dance! You can make up your own routine for you and your friends – just follow the instructions and ideas on the following pages, and then it's time to dance the day away!

Get up and dance!

Making up a dance routine with your friends can be the best fun ever. First, you need to pick a song you'd like to dance to. Think about the rhythm and beat, start moving, and see if you can come up with some steps!

HELLO KITTY TIP

If you're stuck for inspiration, think of your favourite bands. Do they dance in their videos? Maybe that will give you some ideas...

Choose your moves!

There are lots of different dance styles to choose from. Take a look at the ones on these pages, pick your favourite and get moving!

Line Dancing

Line Dancing can be lots of fun, especially with your friends! It works really well with country music, and the steps can be simple to learn.

Disco

Disco music is just made for dancing! And it can be lots of fun to dress up for too. It goes great with pop music, and is lots of fun for parties!

Ballet

Classical music is perfect for ballet dancing. It's very graceful and is beautiful to watch – but it still takes lots of hard work!

Ballroom

Ballroom dancing is best if you can do it with a partner. It can be fast or slow, depending on the music – why not try both and see which you prefer?

Street Dancing

This dancing is super-cool! It's fast and energetic, and can be as crazy as you like, either on your own or with friends. You can even challenge your friends to a dance-off!

Tap

Tap dancing is so much fun! You often see it in old movies, and it's fast and noisy – why not try it on a tiled floor, like in the kitchen or bathroom?

Dancing Tips

- It can be hard to learn dances by heart, but just keep trying and you'll get there. Practice makes perfect!
- You can always write down your dances step by step, and then you can refer to them if you get stuck.
- It also means you can show them to your friends, and they can learn them too!
- If you're stuck for different ideas, why not have everyone make up their own move, and then see if you can put them together to make one super dance?

Hello Kitty loves to dress up, especially for dancing! Why not follow her lead and customise a plain white T-shirt of your own, to join in the fun?

You will need:

A plain white T-Shirt

Ribbons and buttons

Needle and thread

Glue

Scissors

Fabric Paints

ALWAYS ASK A GROWN-UP FOR HELP BEFORE USING SCISSORS!

Design Ideas

Paint a design on your T-shirt with fabric paints! You can do something as complicated as a picture of your favourite band, or as simple as a big star or heart! Or even just try flicking your paintbrush over the T-shirt, to create some cool splatters!

You can make a super-pretty design with ribbons. Just cut the ribbons to length and glue or sew them around the neck and armholes, or tie them into bows and glue them on – gorgeous.

Why not try adding buttons to your T-shirt? You can glue or sew them on. They don't need to match, and you can put them on randomly, or add them in patterns. What about a big star in the middle, made of different sparkly buttons?

Turn the page for a sneak peek at

next adventure...

The Wedding Day

Hello Kitty did a little twirl, and her floaty pink dress spun out around her. It was made up of layers and layers of silky material and topped off with pretty netting – like a pink frothy milkshake! Hello Kitty felt like the perfect princess!

Hello Kitty smiled across the dressmaker's shop to where her twin sister, Mimmy, stood in exactly the same outfit, which was being worked on by the dressmaker. They were both going to be bridesmaids that very weekend and this was their last fitting. Hello Kitty looked around her — rolls of material, ribbons, and trimmings lay scattered around the shop. It was messy, but cosy, just as Hello Kitty liked it.

At that moment an older girl in her twenties came running in through the front door. It was their family friend, Emily, who the girls were going to be bridesmaids for. Hello Kitty's Mama and Papa had known Emily since she was a little girl. Emily had already had the fittings for her wedding dress and she was here to pick it up, while taking a look at the bridesmaids dresses too. Quickly, she called an apology to the dressmaker and hurried over to sit down with Mama.

Hello Kitty smiled. Emily was always late for everything!

Mama White crossed the room and straightened Hello Kitty's dress before smiling at both her daughters and putting a protective arm around Hello Kitty's shoulders.

Hello Kitty peeked a look at Mimmy. After the final fitting today they would actually get to take their dresses home! It was so exciting!

At that moment, the dressmaker stepped away from Mimmy and Hello Kitty, Mama and Emily each let out a little squeal. Hello Kitty had known their dresses were beautiful, but seeing Mimmy in the finished dress, it was even more perfect than she remembered! The dresses were nearly the same as

Emily's wedding dress, except they were pink instead of white. She looked at Mimmy. The dress had little rosebuds running all over it and there was a pretty pearl trim around the neckline. Instead of a long train it had a frothy tulle skirt, and while Emily was wearing a lace veil that cascaded down her back and a sparkly tiara, Hello Kitty and Mimmy had bows with rosebuds on them too. Mimmy did a quick spin. Ta da! Hello Kitty didn't think she had ever seen her looking so pretty...

Out now!

A HELLO KITTY STORY.

HELLO KITTY
and friends

The Wedding Day

Win Hello Kitty Goodies and prizes!

Collect the secret passwords in the first six Hello Kitty and Friends books, and go to **www.harpercollins.co.uk/HelloKittyandFriends** to download your exclusive Hello Kitty activities, games and fun!

Collect all six secret passwords to win super-special goodies!*

Coming soon: